The Tree By The Woodpile

and other

Dene Spirit of Nature Tales

The TREE by the WOODPILE

And other DENE SPIRIT of NATURE TALES

Raymond Yakeleya

*The Tree illustrated by Deborah Desmarais
and Translated by Jane Modeste*

UpRoute
Books & Media

UpRoute Books and Media
An Imprint of Durvile Publications Ltd.
Calgary, Alberta, Canada

Copyright © 2018 by Raymond Yakeleya
'The Tree by the Woodpile' story illustrations © 2018 by Deborah Desmarais
Translation © 2018 Jane Modeste

National Library of Canada Cataloguing in Publications Data
Yakeleya, Raymond 1954 -
The Tree by the Woodpile and other Dene Spirit of Nature Tales

In English and Sahtu Dene
Additional pen and ink illustrations by Paul Weymouth Andrews
Design and art direction by Lorene Shyba

"The Wolf" story previously published in part as "Elder thanks wolf for gift."
Alberta Sweetgrass, Vol. 14, Issue 1, 2006. "By permission of Julie Lennie."

ISBN: 978-1-988824-03-1 (print pbk), | ISBN: 978-1-988824-16-1 (epub)
1. Dene First Nation | 2. First Nations Folklore | 3. Canada
Book One in the Youth 'Spirit of Nature' Series
First edition | Second printing 2018

Information on this title www.durvile.com and www.uproute.ca.

Printed and bound in Canada
Durvile Publications Ltd. gratefully acknowledges the assistance of the
Alberta Government through the Alberta Media Fund. Durvile is a member of Book Publishers
Association of Alberta (BPAA) and the Association of Canadian Publishers (ACP).

This book is dedicated
to the memory of my three grandmothers
Granny Elizabeth Yakeleya,
Granny Harriet Gladue, and
Granny Adele Lennie.

Tulita, Northwest Territories

Tulita is where my stories take place.
In Dene language, Tulita means
"Where the rivers or waters meet."

— Raymond

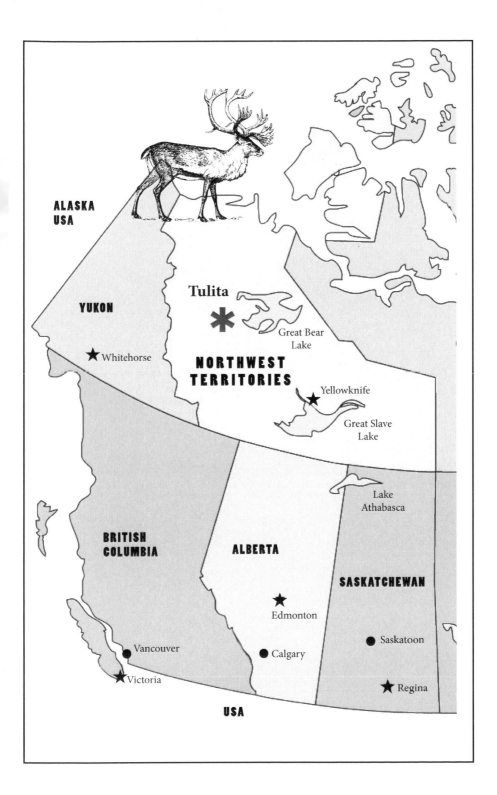

ALASKA
USA

YUKON

★ Whitehorse

Tulita

Great Bear
Lake

NORTHWEST
TERRITORIES

★ Yellowknife

Great Slave
Lake

Lake
Athabasca

BRITISH
COLUMBIA

ALBERTA

SASKATCHEWAN

★ Edmonton

● Saskatoon

● Vancouver

● Calgary

★ Victoria

★ Regina

USA

OUR DENE LANGUAGE

In this book when you see words that look interesting and unusual, those words are in our Dene language. They look like this.

(Tseh deréla ghá edɪre dechį

náɪɔa sį́į suré segha benégǫdɪ.)

These words mean

"The tree by the woodpile
is beautiful to me."

SPIRIT OF NATURE TALES

The Tree By The Woodpile

I love visiting my Granny Elizabeth. To our Dene people, Elders, like my grandmother, teach us the ancient knowledge of our People by telling us our legends and history.

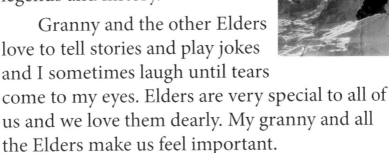

Granny and the other Elders love to tell stories and play jokes and I sometimes laugh until tears come to my eyes. Elders are very special to all of us and we love them dearly. My granny and all the Elders make us feel important.

One winter day last year, outside Granny's log cabin at the hunting camp, she pointed to the old tree beside the woodpile and said,

Dechį ghą́įdá, dene béré ǫt'e.

"You see that tree? That is our food!"

I thought, "How can that tree be our food?"

Now that it is Spring and the snow has melted, I am still puzzled. I look at Granny's old tree, from top to bottom, from side to side and slowly walk around, but I am not at all sure what I am looking for. It is a riddle to me.

Granny looks at me and motions for me to come beside her. Then she says,

Ɂįts'é síį dechį ɔelé ghǫ shétį hǝ́ nakįnę
ɔįts'é kwę́ ghǫ shéts'eyǝ t'á dene béré ǫt'e.

"You see, my boy, the moose eats the leaves of that tree and we eat the moose, so that is our food!"

I nod to her that I am beginning to understand and she continues,

Chįą t'o dechį yíı daweʔǫ sį́į góhtsı kǫ́ ǫt'e. Dléa k'ola eyı nágwə sį́į ts'énǫhjú ghǫ shétį sį́į k'ola bebéré ǫt'e.

"Do you see that nest in the tree? It is the home of the robins and it gives them shelter. Also, the squirrel lives there and he lives on the seeds of the tree, so it is his food too. "

Eyı dechį sį́į ʔįhbé gókǫ́ nįdé dene kə yecha réhkw'ı gots'ę setsə́ə yeyı chooté k'ola kenahdí.

"That tree also gives our People shade in the summer when it gets very hot and I can remember your grandfather having a nap. It made him very happy. "

The wind blows through the leaves and Granny and I listen to the music the leaves make. I decide to climb the tree and Granny looks up, watching me closely.

When finally I climb down from the tree. Granny squeezes my hand and continues in a very soft voice.

Eyı dechı sı̨ı dene hóot'ı̨nę nezǫ́ gudí gogha naédíı k'ola katı̨́.

"That tree also gives our People medicine for their cuts and it helps us to stay healthy."

Dechı sı̨ı begháré ʔehdakánats'udә́ hә́ eghálageda gha yet'á ası̨ı yágíhtsı̨́.

"It gives us wood to make bows and arrows, paddles, boats, snowshoes, and other tools we need to help us survive and to stay alive."

Dene hóot'ı̨nę kә yet'á ʔexele gehtsı sı̨ı bet'á kats'eretı, ts'ejı hә́ dagowә.

"Our People make their drums from that tree, so we pray with them, sing our songs, and dance our dances."

Sah nejı nı̨dé asáode ch'á dechı k'ə dekítɬə.
Tsá k'ola edıre dechı t'á dekı́ gohtsı.

"Even the bears, when they are afraid, especially the young ones, will climb up the tree for safety. The beavers make their houses from this tree and it is also their food. "

My grandmother stops and looks at me to make sure that I am listening. We smile at each other.

"That tree has helped our People find their direction by being a landmark so we do not get lost."

Dechı sı̨ı sadzá láı̨t'e t'á xae k'énahta ayí zá ǫt'e sı̨ı heots'erı̨hshǫ. Ɂı̨hbé k'ə nı̨dé alé ɂı̨t'ǫ́ dekoe at'į́ gháts'eda nı̨dé ekáa xae anagode gha heots'erı̨hshǫ. Det'ǫnę hə́ xah hə́ ekáa areyǫnę́ nadenedə́ gha.

"The tree is like a clock, telling us about the seasons. In the summer, when we see the first yellow leaves, we are being told that fall and then winter is on the way. Ever since springtime, ducks and geese have been getting themselves and their young ones ready for the long flight to the south."

Edıre dechı sı́ı̨ bets'ę tseh t'á kǫ́ ts'eréhk'ǫ́ gogha ǫt'e.

"That tree also gives us wood to make our homes and wood to burn for our fires when we are cold and need to cook our food."

"Other animals like the caribou are also seeing these signs and getting ready for the change of seasons."

Asįį nákə t'a edegha sánégots'íɔa gha sįį la, elígu hə́ shéts'eyə godahk'ə́.

"The People must also prepare for the long visit of our two hard but important teachers, the cold and hunger.

"We must be ready for them as our lives will depend on it. In our land, the weather is the one who is the boss, not us.

"We have to know what to do in order to survive, so we must watch out for the signs that tell us that change is coming. In your life, you must do that also."

Dechį sį̃į zhah deníle were asį̃į nǫde
dene ghánaʔá. ʔįt'ǫ́ dekoe anat'į́, dedele hə
dek'odze at'į́ nįdé begháré kédaorát'į.
Dene areyǫnę́, tıch'ádíı, det'ǫnę hə gonáą
asį̃į dıre nę́nę́ k'ə yágúdí hįlį sį̃į dechį láaní k'ę́
edegoredí. Dene gúhłə́, ts'enazhə dene hejǫ
gots'ę, ʔįt'ǫ́ táretł'é nįdé, eyı láaní k'ę́ dene
k'ę́ dene lǫ agot'į.

"But the tree has one last beautiful
present for us before the snow comes. Leaves
all turn yellow, orange, and red. The bright
colours make everything look so pretty for
one last time. It is the favourite season for
many of our People. An important lesson
to know is that all People, animals, birds,
anything alive in this world, follow the pattern
shown by the trees."

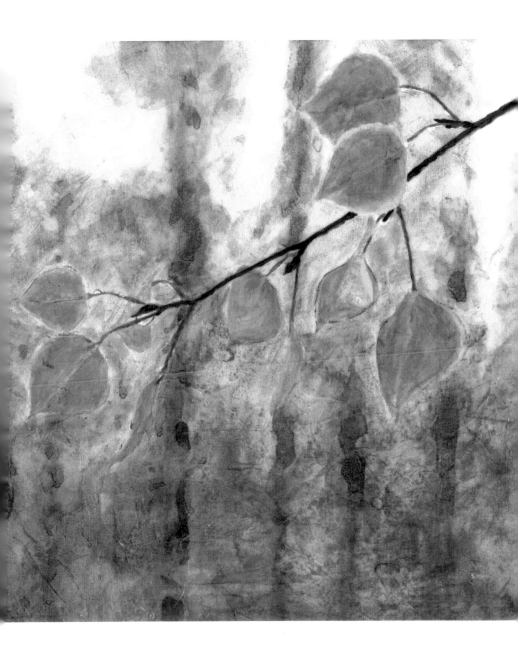

"We are born, grow up, get old and then like the leaves when they fall, we are gone."

Dene dzęnę heretá dene ghǫt'á sį̃ suré
got'áoréꜣá ǫt'e t'á, surí beghǫ
edeséts'erɪht'e gha góꜣǫ. Asį̃ k'ét'ą̃ dene
ghánats'ıꜣá gots'ę dágúꜣǫ́ keots'į́hꜣǫ sį̃
ts'éhꜣǫ́nę nezǫ́ agotsį́hwhę gha góꜣǫ.
Ɂɪt'ǫ́ táretł'é nɪdé beghǫ seyíɪ tseréꜣǫ.
Netsáꜣ dene ghá wíle ekúu keghǫ nahdí
kúlú łá dzęnę beghánats'eda gha.

"Time is a very important gift. We must try
to be wise about what we do with it. We must
always give back to others and try to leave
everything better than the way we found
it. For me, it is with sadness that I watch the
leaves fall down and the tree becomes bare. I
am reminded of all the good people, like your
grandpa, who have left us. One day we will
join them."

Granny Elizabeth looks away for a
moment but then looks back at me with great
kindness and trust. She takes a long, deep
breath and whispers to me.

"My boy, I have been waiting for this
moment as you are my first grandchild and
finally old enough to understand these things
I have been waiting to tell you for a long time."

"There is a God and we call Him *Newet'sine* in our language. *Newet'sine* means *The One Who Made the World.*"

My eyes get very wide. Granny smiles and gives me a little hug before she continues.

"We have known of Him long before the white people and priests came to our lands. *Newet'sine* plays no favourites with his Creation, of which we are part. We cannot see God as I see you but we see God in nature, which is all around us.

"*Newet'sine* expects us to have a heart for all people and to help them. We must especially help Elders, kids with no mom and dad, those in the hospital who are sick and dying, and those with no home and are hungry. We are not to judge anyone as that is *Newet'sine's* job. We are just to help."

She lowers her eyes and together we listen to the wind blowing through the leaves.

"These are the things that are expected of us. You must also know that *Newet'sine* is always with us in all of our life and especially in our darkest and loneliest moments, which comes to all of us, but remember, you are never alone. Talk with him. Get to know Him. It is always special to talk to Him.

"I know this because when I was your age and in the darkest time of my life, I lost my mom and dad and we became orphans. Your uncle, and aunt and I were just kids when this happened and we did not have a home to go to. There is no worse feeling in the world than to not have a home.

"We asked ourselves, 'Where do we go? How will we live?' It is a terrible thing to be an orphan my boy."

She stops her life story for a moment, looks away from me for a long time, and then turns to face me. Her eyes are very sad and tears fall slowly down her face. She wipes away her tears and in a down-hearted, low voice continues.

"I was the oldest, not even ten years old and I did not know what to do with my young brother and sister who looked at me to help them. I did not know what to do. *Newet'sine* helped us but we still had great struggles."

Looking at Granny, I know at that moment what it means to have a broken heart. Her face is wet with tears as she relives this terrible sadness that happened in her life. I start to cry

also, the tears just come to me and I cannot stop
them. Her story spills out of her and we are sad
together. We hug each other. I had never seen
this side of my beautiful grandmother before.
After our hugs, we are soon smiling again.

"It is important for me to tell you these words that will guide your life. My mom and dad never got to tell me these things that I am telling you. That's why this is very important. You will have times in your life where things will not go right and you will fail, and you will fall. This happens to everyone. When you fall, you must get up and keep on going. You must also find why you are here on this world and only you can find that out. *Newet'sine* put us here for a reason.

"As you get to know *Newet'sine*, you will get to know yourself and your purpose. Learn to be kind and how to help. I love to pray, to talk to *Newet'sine*, to share my thoughts with Him, just like talking to my own mom and dad all about my good news and my worries. I ask for guidance, not for anything else. I ask for help for those who need it, and others might ask for help for me when I need it. This is how we make our wishes known. *Newet'sine* always listens and knows, we are never alone.

"I want you to have a love for God and

to know it is always a privilege to talk to Him whenever you want to. Learn to make offerings like your Grandpa did when he travelled on the land and water. Learn to be safe and to give back to the world, not always to take, as we need to look after the Creation for not just for ourselves, but for everyone who lives in the world.

"It is in this way that you will find the light. *Newet'sine* is about love, hope and forgiveness. If you can do things that are correct and right, do them. He will be happy, you will be happy, and the animals will be too.

"Another thing to remember is it really is a beautiful world and a lot of fun. See it and enjoy it with many wonderful people. Do that for yourself and thank *Newet'sine* for this and be safe, and always, always help the People.

"Granny looks at me to see if I am listening, She sees that I am, and she hugs me and kisses me on the forehead. "*Mahsi, mahsi,* my boy for listening to an old lady who loves you." We hold each other for what seems like a long time. This is a very sacred moment with my Granny. "

Granny points back at the tree and says,

Dechı sı̨ı̨ beʔelé wı́le at'í nı̨dé ekáa xae goghá agot'ı̨.
Tseh deréla ghá edıre dechı nájʔa
sı̨ı̨ suré segha benégǫdı. Newehtsı̨nę edıre nę́nę́
wehtsı kúlú detselé ghǫ nétǫ t'á suré xae elı́gu
ch'á yek'ə́dí. Ası̨ı̨ łǫ dene ghálə, gha ǫt'e.

"The tree, when it is bare and alone, is ready for winter. This tree is beautiful to me. It inspires me and I love looking at it in all the seasons. Even *Newet'sine, The One Who Made the World,* loves his trees and watches over them and protects them in the coldest part of the winter. Trees are outside with no parka or jacket to protect them, just their bark, and yet they survive and come back to life every year with their green leaves. They have so many gifts for us."

I am in awe, as I have no idea my grandmother thinks like this. Granny smiles and says.

"The trees coming back to life every year is like a real miracle to me."

Asįį suré godaréhcho dechı hehtsı la edıre dene
dazhı begháré ts'ejú hehtsı ǫt'e.
Kaarehtı táonéht'é senewehtsınę edıre dechı
ghǫ máhsı hérehsı zo. Newehtsınę areyǫnę́
yéhtsı hılı sį́į bets'erįhchá gha góʔǫ, eyı hǝ
suré bek'ǝts'edí hǝ kúukare tséts'ıhwhı hǝ
bénáots'eyǝ gha ǫt'éle.

"Another very important thing that this
tree does is that it makes the air we breathe.
If it was not for that, we would not be alive,
so I always include a few words in my prayers,
thanking *Newet'sine* for the trees."

Looking straight at me now she says,

"Grandpa used to say that we must respect
everything that is made by *Newet'sine* and
look after things without destroying them for
nothing, and never waste anything. Grandpa
would say that we must have special respect
for female animals when they have their young
babies, as they are our future. You must care
for everything, as the People, the animals and
nature all live together in this world. We People
cannot survive by ourselves alone. We need the
Creation to help us to survive.

36

"The animals and nature do not need us for anything, but we need them for everything to be alive. We must take care of all we touch and treat nature with respect. My boy, you must remember these things that I am telling you. It is in this way that we show our love, respect and honour to *Newet'sine* for all that He has made. Keep this knowledge as it will guide you in your life. When you get older, pass this knowledge along to your brothers, sisters, friends, children and others, even in other places. I hope they will also pass this knowledge along. It is to help everyone. These words will always be good."

I cannot find anything to say, so I nod. I understand. Granny gives me a big hug and kisses my head. I hug her too.

With her arms around me she says,

Bebí nelı ekúu nenǫ hə netá hə názé gélə nıdé
netsəə hə sınę hə, nek'əədí nıdé
sure nakegha nezǫ dúwə́.

"The last thing I want to tell you about the tree happened when you were just a baby. Your grandfather and I loved taking care of you while your parents were out hunting."

Ɂehtsəə sį́į tł'uh hə dechį t'á dahbılé negha
wehtsį t'á dáréhwhá gots'ę́ suré nezǫ́
nek'ídí hə nénágúyə. Sįnę hə netsəə hə náarídló
anakįhɔį. Edıre dechį sį́į suré łǫ́
begháré súdı ts'įlə ǫt'e.

"Grandpa got some rope and some wood
and made you a swing and we took turns
playing with you on that swing for hours. I
can still hear the sounds in my head of you
and grandpa laughing. When I look at that
tree, those happy memories and sounds all
come back to me. It's just like that big tree
was a big toy to you along with all its other
important jobs. This tree sure brought us a lot
of happiness."

When Spring comes around all over again, Granny makes me feel important by being with me. We watch the skies come alive with thousands of ducks and geese returning to the North. The animals sense this great change coming all over the land. Even the sun celebrates with us, bringing long days with beautiful pink, red and golden sunsets.

Birds are busy making their nests and singing at all hours. Squirrels are happily making a racket and running around all over the trees. The ponds are awake all night with the sounds of croaking frogs while the beavers and muskrats swim around in the open water, visiting each other.

Newehtsįnę ayíi areyǫnę́ wehtsį sį́į gotí suré beghǫ néetǫ hǝ́ nezǫ́ bek'ǝnedí hederǫtsíle.

Hugging me and looking at me, my grandmother says softly,

"My boy, remember to always love and take care of all that *Newest'sine* has made."

41

The Wolf

My Uncle Alfred told me a story I will never forget. It was about when he was a trapper and a guide in the Northwest Territories, about eighty kilometers northeast of Tulita, at a place called Lennie Lake. He lived with my aunt Julie and my cousins Wilfred, Bertha, and Joanne in a log cabin, nestled in the mountains along the lakeside. Quite often, he said, they would see wolf packs hunting and travelling down the lake. He would take his rifle and load it with a few shells and would shoot a few wolves but one day, as he explained it, a lone wolf changed his life. This is his story, just as he told it to me.

Uncle told me ... "Early one morning, I looked through my frost-covered window and there he was, a lone, big, silver wolf. Quickly, I

dressed in my parka, grabbed my rifle and shells, jumped on my snowmobile, and raced after him. The wolf saw me, and he headed out across the lake. He was almost all the way out to the bushes when I raised my rifle and shot.

"I could not miss. My rifle gave him a sure shot right in the stomach, but he disappeared into the bushes. I could not pursue him because the snow was too deep. This meant that I must return to my cabin for my snowshoes. Upon my return to the spot where I had shot the wolf, I put on my snowshoes and began to follow the bloody footprints into the bushed area. Just as I entered the bush I could see him lying under some low-lying branches. He also saw me.

"The wolf jumped up and ran back toward the frozen lake. He was heading for a high drift of snow. I made my way back to my snowmobile, jumped on and was in pursuit of the wolf again. I chased him to the Willow Point where he stopped, turned, and stood on a high drift of snow. He weakly stood looking out over the lake, having lost a lot of blood. He watching both sides of the lake, realizing that there was no way to escape. I stopped my snowmobile and watched him. He looked straight at me, looking me square in the eyes. I could feel him questioning my actions as if to say, 'Why are you doing this to me?'

"My heart felt heavy and sad but I had no choice. He was wounded and suffering and it would not be fair to let him suffer more. I had to end his life. This is something I am not proud about. For this action, I am ashamed of myself but I am telling you this so you and others will not hurt an animal for no reason.

"With a sad heart, I knelt down beside the beautiful, mysterious animal. There in the snow, my thoughts wandered back in time to when I was a young boy and I'd had a very powerful dream of a wolf. In this dream, I was playing along the Mackenzie River when I spotted a pack of wolves travelling together. Suddenly, one of the wolves left the pack and approached me. I was afraid until the wolf began to speak to me. He said, 'Do not be afraid, I only want to share something with you.' He showed me a pair of snowshoes and when I looked at them, they were laced differently than how my People laced snowshoes. I realized that the wolf was showing me how to lace the snowshoes in a new way. When I awoke from my dream, I knew that the wolf had shown me how to be a better hunter in my youth. He'd given me a gift to use and share with my People.

"My thoughts returned to the moment at hand and I continued to stroke the silver-furred wolf. I felt ashamed for taking this wolf's life. One of his relatives, or maybe even himself, had been the one who had shown me the way to be a better hunter. I knew it was time to repay the wolf that had helped me provide food and clothing for my family. It was time to thank the wolf for sharing his knowledge with me so long ago. I knew right then and there that I would never hunt another wolf.

"I spent a few more years in the bush and I never hunted another wolf. I learned to respect the wolf and in return, they respected me and never bothered me or my traps after that. There is so much that humans can learn from the wolf. Wolves are very wise animals.

"An old man once told me, 'You must treat the animals with respect and never infringe upon their ways, animals can teach us many valuable lessons.' The wolf taught me a very important lesson. They are so much like us and have lessons to share, but we must listen to them."

•••

Those were the words told to me by my Uncle Alfred about appreciating wild animals' thoughts and feelings and I now share them with you to remember to respect animals as a spirit of nature.

The Mountain, the Wind and the Wildflowers

The mountain stands before us. Not just any mountain, but Bear Rock Mountain, the special mountain of legend of my People, the Dene of the Northwest Territories. On this summer morning, my friends and I set out to climb the mountain for the first time. All my life, since I can remember, I have wanted to climb this mountain and so have my friends. Every day and in all the seasons, from our town of Tulita, we admire the mountain it in all its beauty. The day has finally come when we are old enough to cross the blue waters of the Bear River to take on the challenge of climbing Bear Rock Mountain.

My mother has told me about how she, her
cousins, and her friends climbed Bear Rock
Mountain when they were about my age. I have
always loved her stories about how she visited
two lakes on top of the mountain and a little
cave. I want to see these lakes and the cave for
myself, and my friends are curious too. Mother
remembers the trail well enough to describe
to us how to carefully walk along the face of
the mountain, and then how to follow the trail
upwards to the top, and beyond.

The sun is high in the sky, hot and getting
hotter as we start our climb. Each of us has
some canned food and water in our pack sacks.
There are several tricky spots as we begin the
slippery climb, but together we figure things

out. The rock-strewn trail takes us higher and higher up the mountain. We are so hot that salty sweat pours off us, but we do not stop. As we climb higher and higher, we notice that we can see much further into the mountains to the west because of the horizon becomes so large.

Suddenly we see an eagle's nest on the side of the mountain, all big sticks tangled up together in a big circle, as is their building style. We talk about how eagles might have soared up there for thousands of years, for maybe as long as the mountain itself. If the nest could talk, it would tell of things that we can only imagine. We don't see the eagle but we know she is watching us.

Finally, after a very long climb, we burst onto the top of Bear Rock Mountain to a spectacular sight. The cool wind hits us, and the silence too. We do not say anything to each other at that moment, but together we observe what the eagle sees from on high — lots and lots of forests, rivers, and mountains.

For me, it is a very special feeling of accomplishment to climb the mountain, especially since it is our first time. We are all silently happy and proud of ourselves. We are sweaty, thirsty, dusty, and mosquito-bitten but in this moment we are on top of the world.

We still have another stretch of hiking to the valley of the lakes. The valley is easy to find because my mom told us to watch out for a unique structure of high rocks. The lakes, nestled in a small valley surrounded by stone walls, are a beautiful sight to behold, and we talk about how good it will feel to jump into the cold black water. Collecting a bit of firewood along the way, we make our way down to the main lake where we, first of all, take time to lay out a circle of stones and make a little fire. We respect fire as a spirit of nature so we always make sure it burns good and safe.

Once we are sure the fire is burning safely, we run down to the waters edge, tear off our clothes down to our underwear, and dive into the cold and clear black water of the lake. It feels so great! We swim and splash around for a few minutes but cannot stay in the cold water for very long. We jump out all nice and clean and gather around our small fire, shivering and chattering our teeth.

We open up our cans of beans and meat with our hunting knives, steel cutting steel, and our food is soon bubbling all over in the cans in the fire, nice and hot. We make short work of the food and it disappears in no time, except for the little bits we give back to the fire. This is our way of saying 'thank you' to to the spirit of the flames for giving us its heat. Then we spread ourselves out on our towels on the ground, faces to the sun, smiling and happy.

My friends decide to take a nap so on my own, I walk along the shore to enjoy the surroundings and the silence. On the way, I notice a pink flower and lean down to look at it more closely. At that moment I notice other flowers of many different colours, scattered all over the place. I have never paid much attention to flowers before, except to pick dandelions and put them in a glass jar and bring them into the house for my mom. I draw myself even closer to the pink flower in order to smell its wild perfume. The flower is perfect in beauty and design, from its red and pink petals to its golden stamen and, of course, the glorious scent. I then look over to observe a blue flower and then a yellow one, and enjoy them in the same way. The flowers all have different shapes, sizes, colours, and perfume.

I look into the blue sky and wonder about the God who has made the world, and these beautiful wildflowers. Who is this God the Creator, who I have heard the Elders call *Newet'sine*. I wonder this to myself and wish to know more about the mysterious being who has made these things, from the highest mountains to the smallest insect. I do not see God as I see another person, but believe with all of my heart that He exists.

I am reminded of a talk I had with my Granny Harriet one day when we walked together along the banks of Bear River, just her and me. That day, I had questioned the existence of God the Creator, asking her, "Why do we never see *Newet'sine*?" Granny answered, "My grandchild, what you are asking is good, as it means you want to learn about things that are not easy to explain. However, I will try."

"When we talk about *Newet'sine*, our God, we have to remember that all life comes from one place. We people love God above all things, even more than our own lives. We trust that everything happens for a reason, even though we cannot understand why things happen the way they do. The reason is often not clear until much later."

She stopped walking for a moment, briefly glanced at me, then continued, looking towards the mountains across the Bear River.

"Have you ever seen the wind?" she asked.

"No," I answered.

"Do you believe there is such a thing as the wind?"

"Yes," I replied.

"Why?" she wanted to know.

"Because I know the wind when it is on my face. When I am warm, it cools me down, and in the winter it makes me feel colder."

She turned and looked at me and smiled and said, "*Newet'sine* is like that. We can't see Him as we see each other but His spirit is in nature — the flowers, the animals, and even you and me. In all these things we can see His work, His touch, His mind, and His power. He is always with us even when we think there is no one there for us. We are made with His love and by His will. Everything is made like that. He cares for everything that He has made.

"When we do something wrong and we think we are smart because no one has seen us, it is not true. We are being watched and it is He who is watching, so we must do what is right, always. It is to Him that we must answer for all the wrong that we do. Sometimes we make mistakes in our life, but we must always try to do what is right. We must also try to not judge people, but instead try to help when we can. This is very important, maybe the very most important thing. We must try to help everyone, especially strangers. When someone who we don't know comes to our house, we always ask them if they are hungry and if they are, we feed them and give them tea. That is our way.

"I want you and all of my grandchildren to be like that. I love you all and want you to do what you want to do, but to always remember that helping people, young and old, is very important to the God who has created us. What good is it when we eat well but others have nothing to eat and suffer in life? How can we feel good about ourselves if we don't do anything when we should be helping?

"We must be kind. That is why we share, so everyone will have something. Even if it's only a little bit, it's better than nothing. Maybe it will be our turn someday to have nothing to eat and what if nobody helps us? How would that make us feel? Our people share good and bad times together. It is how we show our love to each other. We support each other in these times. It is our way."

It was as if Granny was there with me, but at the present moment, I look west towards the lake shore, wondering if my friends have woken up from their naps. As I walk back through the field of flowers towards our little campsite, I pick one each of the pink, blue, and yellow flowers and remember one more thing that Granny Harriet had told me.

"Our people used to die of starvation in the old days, especially in the mountains in the winter, so sharing is very important to us. We do not want to see that happen again to anyone. Many people died because of hunger when it was cold and animals were hard to get. Our Elders told us that even when that happened, our People never blamed *Newet'sine*, but accepted what was happening. They would stand up with their last strength and face the sun and sky and thank Him for giving them the time to be alive and also to express their love for the Creator one last time. They would then fall into the snow and die with their love and belief in God. Their hearts were not hard. They were not afraid of God and of death because they knew they would be with Him and that this was part of life. It makes me so sad to think of this, my grandchild, but you have to know this and the ones following you must also know this. How many times I have said my prayers for those who suffered with no one to help them? These beliefs are part of us."

I remember that after she told me about these sad things, she turned towards me and smiled, saying, " Just because you can't see something doesn't mean it's not real, like the wind. But I want to remind you to say a prayer of gratitude every day, it never hurts to do this. Talk to God, even when you don't know what to say. Say that you want to tell Him that you love Him and want nothing for yourself. Speak with truth and honesty. He always listens to everything in your heart and in your mind."

Finally she said, "Money means nothing to *Newet'sine*. What is important to Him is what is in our hearts and our actions of what we do. I have my faith in Him always. I know that when we have a big storm with lots of black clouds, rain, wind, thunder, and lightning and when the sun is nowhere to be seen, the sun is still there, hidden maybe, but still there, like *Newet'sine*."

Smiling at me again she said, "I am telling you these things, but look to find the truth in your life for yourself. No one can live our lives for us. Your number one rule is love God. Everything comes from that."

I look at the flowers in my hand and I silently thank *Newet'sine* for allowing me to pick a few of them, all the while thinking of my grandmother's wise words. I had made a wonderful discovery about the beauty of flowers, and all for free. *Newet'sine* is a true artist in His heart. I can see that for myself.

I walk slowly down to the shore of the lake and I can see that my friends are just now waking up from their nap. I bring the flowers to my face to smell them one last time and then throw them up into the air to scatter them onto the lake, knowing they will live longer in the water. A soft wind touches my face and hair as I watch the pink, blue and yellow flowers float away. Then, before I go back to join my friends, I bow my head.

Since it is getting late in the afternoon, we decide to go to the little cave another day. We take our time on the way back down, walking high along on the skyline, refreshed, and relaxed. The slow pace makes me think and reflect and I realize that *Newet'sine*, mysterious as always, is very real and that we are lucky to be here in this world. My cherished grandmothers have told me, "Life is precious, so let us use our time wisely."

I look across the horizon, and for a moment I thank the One who gave me my precious life. Then my friends and I look out over the steep drop of the mountain and then run down fearlessly, yelling at the top of our lungs, "*Hoo, hoo!*" We feel its great to be alive.

GRANNY ELIZABETH

This is my Granny Elizabeth. She told me many things about Dene life and teachings, as you have read in "The Tree by the Woodpile" story. She said that we must know that *Newet'sine* is always with us in all of our life and especially in our darkest and loneliest moments, which come to all of us. She told me to remember that we are never alone because we can talk with Him. It is because of Granny Elizabeth that I came to understand that a simple tree can also be our food, shelter, and medicine. *Mahsi* Granny.

UNCLE ALFRED

Uncle Alfred was the fun and mischievous uncle of the Lennie Family of Tulita. I believe he was the one to name me Raymond after a friend of his who had died in a accident. He took a interest in me and other cousins and tried to teach us things that traditional men would do on the land. He took me and my cousin Ernie on our first moose hunt when I was about 12 years old at Kelly Lake, a experience I will never forget. He constantly talked to us, teaching us and doing it all the while with humour and laughter. *Mahsi* Uncle.

GRANNY HARRIET

Granny Harriet was a Mountain Dene
woman and midwife for the Tulita
People, which means she helped
mothers bring babies into the world.
She brought my mother into the world
and also brought me into the world.
Granny Harriet was a spiritual woman
and always tried to live in the right way
with kindness and gratitude. She did not
talk a lot, but on occasion had deep and
thoughtful things to say in order to teach
us the ways of *Newet'sine* and ways of the
Dene People. *Mahsi* Granny.

DEBORAH DESMARAIS

Deborah painted the beautiful artwork on canvas for "The Tree" story and also for the cover of the book. She is an artist and lives in Calgary, Alberta.

JANE MODESTE

Jane translated "The Tree" story into the Sahtu Dene language. Jane lives in Deline in the Northwest Territories and works hard to preserve and teach traditional knowledge and language.

ME — RAYMOND YAKELEYA

I, Raymond, am originally from Tulita in Northwest Territories but now I live in Edmonton, Alberta. My job is that I write, direct, and produce documentary films like *The Last Mooseskin Boat,* which was with the National Film Board of Canada. I think that with the passing of many of our Elders, like my Granny Elizabeth and Granny Harriet and my Uncle Alfred, telling our Dene People's stories is more important now than ever before. I hope to inspire and encourage Elders and young native people to proudly write down their own stories to create a voice for our People.